This book belongs to:

. . . .

To Justin. Sleep peacefully. A.S.

For the very patient Spencer, Theo and Tegan. L.M.

OXFORD
UNIVERSITY PRESS

Great Clarendon Street, Oxford OX2 6DP

Oxford University Press is a department of the University of Oxford.
It furthers the University's objective of excellence in research, scholarship,
and education by publishing worldwide in

Oxford New York

Auckland Cape Town Dar es Salaam Hong Kong Karachi
Kuala Lumpur Madrid Melbourne Mexico City Nairobi
New Delhi Shanghai Taipei Toronto

With offices in
Argentina Austria Brazil Chile Czech Republic France Greece
Guatemala Hungary Italy Japan Poland Portugal Singapore
South Korea Switzerland Thailand Turkey Ukraine Vietnam

British Library Cataloguing in Publication Data available

ISBN: 978-0-19-278026-3 (paperback)

10 9 8 7 6 5 4 3 2 1

Printed in China

The bedtime story Daddy and Toast are sharing in this book is *Just Like Tonight* by Amber Stewart and Layn Marlow. ISBN: 978-0-19-272850-0

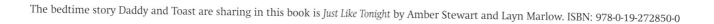

Amber Stewart & Layn Marlow

How Many Sleeps?

OXFORD
UNIVERSITY PRESS

Toast woke early one morning.
He knew that something exciting was going
to happen, and it was going to happen soon.

He could smell it in the quiet morning air,
in the mist still hugging the ground,
in the autumn leaves trembling on
the branches ready to tumble
a golden blanket over the wood.

Toast watched, waiting for
the first leaf to fall . . .

because when the first leaf fell,
that meant it was nearly his birthday.

'How many sleeps till
my birthday?' he asked,
as Mummy tucked him in.

'Too many to start
counting now,'
smiled Mummy.

'How many sleeps till my birthday?'
Toast asked the next night,
and the next,

until one night Mummy said,
'Just enough sleeps to deliver
party invitations to all
your friends.'

So the next day that is exactly what they did.

They delivered
invitations all the way
from Little Hollow . . .

to Big Oak Tree . . .

to Rabbit, Mole, and
Squirrel Red Tail.

'How many sleeps till my birthday now, Mummy?' murmured Toast, so tired from his long walk.

'Just enough sleeps to go collecting party treats,' whispered Mummy.

After breakfast, they gathered
armfuls of gold and rubies, and
special leaves for wrapping.

'How many sleeps till my birthday,
from this exact moment?' Toast wondered,
right in the middle of his bedtime story.

'Exactly enough sleeps to help
Mummy decorate the cake,' said Daddy.

In the morning, Mummy and Toast
picked petals and berries
and nuts for the cake.

Then together they decorated it
so that it was the best birthday cake
Toast had ever seen.

In bed, each evening, Toast lay dreaming
of invitation delivering, of party treats,
of birthday cake, and of what his
present might be.

And each evening Daddy wondered,
quite worriedly, 'How many more
sleeps until Toast's birthday?'

'Just enough, I'm sure,'
Mummy always said,
secretly crossing her fingers.

'Guess how many sleeps now, Toast?'
said Mummy one morning.
'How many?' wailed Daddy.

'Just enough to wrap the party treats,
put the candles on the cake,
and get an extra special early night . . .'

'But that means —' squeaked Toast,
'that means — my birthday is tomorrow!'

And it was.

And there was easily enough time to love
the gifts, play the party games, and eat up
all the cake. And, best of all . . .

time for Toast to open a very special present

and let all his friends share in the fun.

When Toast's day had drawn to an
end — and he was giving Daddy
a hug — he whispered dreamily,
'How many sleeps till my next birthday?'

'Just enough sleeps for Daddy
to start on your next present,'
Mummy whispered back.

But Toast was already asleep.